"Pleeease!" said Sophie.

Mum sighed. "All right. You can look at one more book. Then go straight to sleep."

Sophie grabbed
her favourite
book –

and gasped as a strong
wind swept her away . . .

. . . on a flying carpet!

She was soaring through millions of stars when she spotted some camels, plodding over the sand dunes. A group of people were racing along a path. Sophie swooped down to take a closer look.

She followed the people to a market square, and
held her breath as a young man picked up a magic lamp.
She was about to shout, "Be careful!"
when the wind blew her up and away.

It seemed to be calling
her name as it swirled about . . .

"Sophie! . . .
Sophie!"

"Bedtime!" said Mum.

Sophie sighed. She wasn't sleepy at all. She put her book away and climbed into bed . . .

. . . just for a moment.

Then, very quietly,
she tiptoed out and picked
up another book.

She found herself tumbling
into the strangest world she'd ever seen.

A white rabbit scampered by as fast as his paws
could carry him – and a girl in a blue dress chased
him down a rabbit hole! A big cat grinned
as Sophie set off after them.

Then a voice
called out from
a clump of mushrooms . . .

"Sophie!"

The tallest mushroom
leaned towards her.
"Didn't Mum tell you
to turn off the light?"

“I just needed one more story,”
Sophie said to her dad.

“Time to sleep,” said Dad.

He switched off the light,
and Sophie climbed under
the covers . . .

. . . with her torch – and another book!

It was pitch
dark under the trees.
Fireflies danced around her, and
animals squeaked and growled in
the branches. Suddenly Sophie
heard a deep rumbly

Grrrrr!

An
enormous tiger
chased her through
the jungle . . .

. . . and all the way
to the living room!

Mum and Dad gave her a cuddle and assured her that there were definitely no tigers in her bedroom.

"Let's read one last story," said Mum, "then you really must go to sleep."

Mum took Sophie
back to bed.

Then she
picked up
a tiny little
book, and
began to
read.

Sophie snuggled down into
the warm feathers of a swallow.
Flowers twinkled like stars, and the
bird hummed a tune as it flew. A soft
breeze ruffled its wings – and Sophie
drifted off to sleep.

Sophie's mum smiled,
and tiptoed out of the room.
"At last!" she said.

She was looking forward to reading her own bedtime story. She climbed under the covers, picked up her book . . .

. . . and found herself trekking
along a huge glacier.

She had to reach the
research lab before sundown.
She was about to set off when
a troop of penguins
waddled past.

Then a little penguin
in pyjamas looked up at
her, and said . . .